W9-DES-558

For my Godson,
Lucas Gabriel

Text copyright © 1992 by Ann Jungman
Illustrations copyright © 1992 by Linda Birch
All rights reserved

Published by Bell Books
Boyds Mills Press, Inc.
A Highlights Company
910 Church Street
Honesdale, Pennsylvania 18431

Publisher Cataloging-in-Publication Data
Jungman, Ann.
When the people are away / by Ann Jungman ; [illustrations by]
Linda Birch.—1st American edition.
[32]p. : col. ill. ; cm.
Originally published by PictureLions, an imprint of HarperCollins Publishers, in London, 1992.
Summary: When the people leave home for a holiday, their cats have a party.
ISBN 1-56397-202-6
1. Cats—Juvenile fiction. [1. Cats—Fiction.] I. Birch, Linda, ill.
II. Title.
[E]—dc20   1993
The Library of Congress Catalog Card Number can be obtained from the publisher upon request.

The text of this book is set in 18-point Galliard.
The illustrations are done in watercolors.
Distributed by St. Martin's Press
Printed in Great Britain

10 9 8 7 6 5 4 3 2 1

When The People Are Away

ANN JUNGMAN ~ LINDA BIRCH

NOV 0 4 2011

BELL BOOKS
BOYDS MILLS PRESS

The children stood in the driveway and cried.
"What's wrong?" asked Mom. "Don't you want to visit Grandma?"
"Yes," sniffed the boys, "but what about the cats? Will they be all right without us?"
"Don't worry," said Mom. "I've arranged for your cousin Sandra to feed them. You'll be all right, won't you, cats?"
The two ginger cats sat in the driveway and blinked at Mom.
"Come on, boys," she said. "We'll be back in a few days."

"Well," said Magnus, "that got rid of them for a while."
"I'll miss them," said Lulu.
"Nonsense," replied Magnus. "You know what they say—
'when the cat's away, the mice will play.' "
"But, Magnus, we haven't gone away, and there aren't any
mice."
"Well, I've changed the saying a bit, Lulu. Now it's 'when
the people are away, the cats will play,' " Magnus told her.
"We'll play something different each night. Tonight we're
going to have a dance party. Go and spread the word."

So later that night, all the cats in the neighborhood trooped into Magnus and Lulu's house.

There was lots of loud music, and the cats danced all night.

The cats slept all the next day. They didn't even hear Sandra when she came to feed them.

When Magnus and Lulu woke up, Lulu asked, "What are we going to do tonight?"
"Tonight," Magnus informed her, "we are going to have an all-night video show. Go and spread the word."

So that night the cats gathered and watched cartoons.
"It's 'Tom and Jerry,' " Magnus told them. "You all
know what to do."
So the cats cheered every time Tom, the cat, came on but
booed when Jerry, the mouse, came on.
The cats really enjoyed themselves.

The next evening Lulu asked again,
"What are we going to do tonight, Magnus?"
"An all-night all-in wrestling competition," Magnus
told her. "Go and spread the word."

That night all the cats turned up looking very tough.
Magnus made them form two lines.
"Everyone is to wrestle with the cat opposite him or
her," he said. "The winners will fight each other."

So the cats had great fun wrestling with each other. In the end Magnus won. "Magnus is the champ," they cried.

The next day Lulu asked, "Can we have a night off? I'm very tired."

"Certainly not," said Magnus. "The people will be back soon. Tonight is the Great Cat-Singing Contest. Go on, go and spread the word."

That night the cats arrived looking very excited.

"You musn't sing too loudly," Magnus told them.
"People don't like the sound of cats singing, though
I don't know why."
"We'll be very quiet," promised the cats.
So the cats each sang in turn. They were very good.
But the best was Lulu. She sang and played the guitar.
It was a sad song and everyone cried.

The next day Magnus looked at the calendar.
"Our people are coming back," he told Lulu. "This is our last night."
"Can we have another singing contest?" asked Lulu hopefully.
"No," said Magnus. "Tonight we will have a grand midnight feast. Spread the word. Everyone is to bring something to eat and no cans. We're tired of that."

So one cat brought a carton of cream,

another brought two sardines,

one brought some liver,

another brought chicken, and one brought some shrimp.

"What a feast we are going to have," said Magnus.

That night the cats ate and ate until there was nothing left.

A big black cat stood up on the piano. "Friends, friends," he cried. "To Magnus and Lulu, our hosts and friends. May their people go away very often."

"To Magnus and Lulu and their people," chorused all the cats.

"Thanks," said Magnus.

"Speech, speech," cried the cats.

Magnus climbed up on the piano.

"Friends," he said. "Fellow cats, we've all had lots of fun. Now, as you know, our people are coming back. Please help us with the cleaning up, so that no one knows what has been happening. That way we can do it again."

Soon, two of the cats were loading the dishwasher,

another three pushed the vacuum cleaner around with difficulty, two others tidied up, someone dusted, and another polished the silver.

By morning no one could have known that the cats had had:

A dance party,

a wrestling competition,

an all-night video session,

a singing contest,

and a midnight feast.

As soon as the children got back, they rushed into the house to find Magnus and Lulu. "Did you miss us a lot?" they asked, giving both cats a hug.

But Magnus and Lulu just stretched and yawned and then curled up in their basket and went back to sleep.

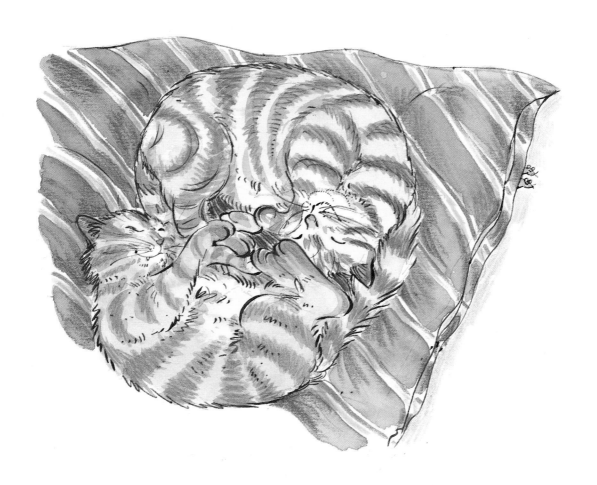